A Note to Parents and Caregivers

With a focus on math, science, of content information and the the development of problem-sol

 The PURPLE LEVEL presents basic topics and objects using high frequency words and simple language patterns.

 The RED LEVEL presents familiar topics using common words and repeating sentence patterns.

 The BLUE LEVEL presents new ideas using a larger vocabulary and varied sentence structure.

 The YELLOW LEVEL presents more challenging ideas, a broad vocabulary, and wide variety in sentence structure.

 The GREEN LEVEL presents more complex ideas, an extended vocabulary range, and expanded language structures.

 The ORANGE LEVEL presents a wide range of ideas and concepts using challenging vocabulary and complex language structures.

When sharing a content focused book with your child, read to find out facts and concepts, pausing often to restate and talk about the new information. The realistic story format provides an opportunity to talk about the language used, and to learn about reading to problem-solve for information. Encourage children to measure, make maps, and consider other situations that allow them to apply what they are learning.

There is no right or wrong way to share books with children. Find time to read and share new learning with your child, and pass on the legacy of literacy.

Adria F. Klein, Ph.D.
Professor Emeritus
California State University
San Bernardino, California

Editor: Julie Gassman
Designer: Hilary Wacholz
Art Director: Heather Kindseth
Managing Editor: Christianne Jones
The illustrations in this book were created digitally.

Picture Window Books
A Capstone Imprint
151 Good Counsel Drive
P.O. Box 669
Mankato, MN 56002-0669
877-845-8392
www.capstonepub.com

Copyright © 2009 by Picture Window Books
All rights reserved. No part of this book may be reproduced without written permission from the publisher. The publisher takes no responsibility for the use of any of the materials or methods described in this book, nor for the products thereof.

Printed in the United States of America in North Mankato, Minnesota.
032010
005747R

 All books published by Picture Window Books are manufactured with paper containing at least 10 percent post-consumer waste.

Library of Congress Cataloging-in-Publication Data
Aboff, Marcie.
Counting on a win/by Marcie Aboff; illustrated by Len Epstein.
p. cm. — (Read-it! readers. Math)
Includes bibliographical references.
ISBN 978-1-4048-5251-8 (hardcover)
ISBN 978-1-4048-5252-5 (paperback)
[1. Money—Fiction. 2. Fairs—Fiction.] I. Epstein, Len, ill. II. Title.
PZ7.A164Cou 2009
[E]—dc22
                                            2008032390

COUNTING ON A WIN

by Marcie Aboff
illustrated by Len Epstein

Special thanks to our advisers for their expertise:

Stuart Farm, M.Ed., Mathematics Lecturer
University of North Dakota

Adria F. Klein, Ph.D.
Professor Emeritus, California State University
San Bernardino, California

PICTURE WINDOW BOOKS
Minneapolis, Minnesota

Jody, Max, and Greg were on vacation with their parents.

Every day, they walked down to the boardwalk. That's where all the games were.

Jody and her brothers waited in line at the ticket booth. The tickets cost one quarter each.

Jody gave the man one dollar. The man gave Jody four tickets.

"I want Freddy the frog!" cried Max.
"Please win me Freddy!"

Jody had promised Max she would win him a stuffed frog. That was five days ago. They were leaving tomorrow.

"I'll try, Max," she said.

They walked up to the basketball game.
Freddy the frog was one of the prizes.
"I could make a basket," said Jody.

She gave the man at the booth two tickets. Jody looked at the hoop. She aimed the basketball.

Whoosh! The ball went in!

Max jumped up and clapped. "I'll take Freddy!" Jody said.

"You have to get the ball in the basket twice for Freddy," said the man behind the booth.

Jody aimed the ball again. This time she missed.

The man behind the booth gave Jody a stuffed basketball.

"Here you go, Max. You can play with the ball," Jody said.

"I want Freddy!" Max said.

"Maybe I can win him tonight," Jody said. "Let's go get some ice cream."

"I'll buy the ice-cream cones," Greg said. Each cone cost one dollar.

Greg took out a one-dollar bill, four quarters, five dimes, and ten nickels. That was enough for all three ice-cream cones.

Four quarters	=	$1.00 (one dollar)
Five dimes	=	50¢
Ten nickels	=	50¢
50¢ + 50¢	=	$1.00

Later that day, Jody counted the money in her right pocket. She had a one-dollar bill and five nickels. She had one dollar and twenty-five cents in her right pocket.

Five nickels = One quarter

Then Jody took the money out of her left pocket. She had a fifty-cent piece. She also had four dimes and ten pennies. That was another fifty cents. With the money from her right pocket, she had a total of two dollars and twenty-five cents.

Four dimes = 40¢
Ten pennies = 10¢

Later the whole family went on rides. They played some games, too. They won lots of prizes, but nobody won Freddy the frog.

Jody felt bad that no one had won Freddy the frog, but she didn't have much money left. She had already spent two dollars on the games.

She checked her pocket. She had five pennies, two nickels, and one dime left.

That was twenty-five cents, or one quarter. It was just enough for one more ticket!

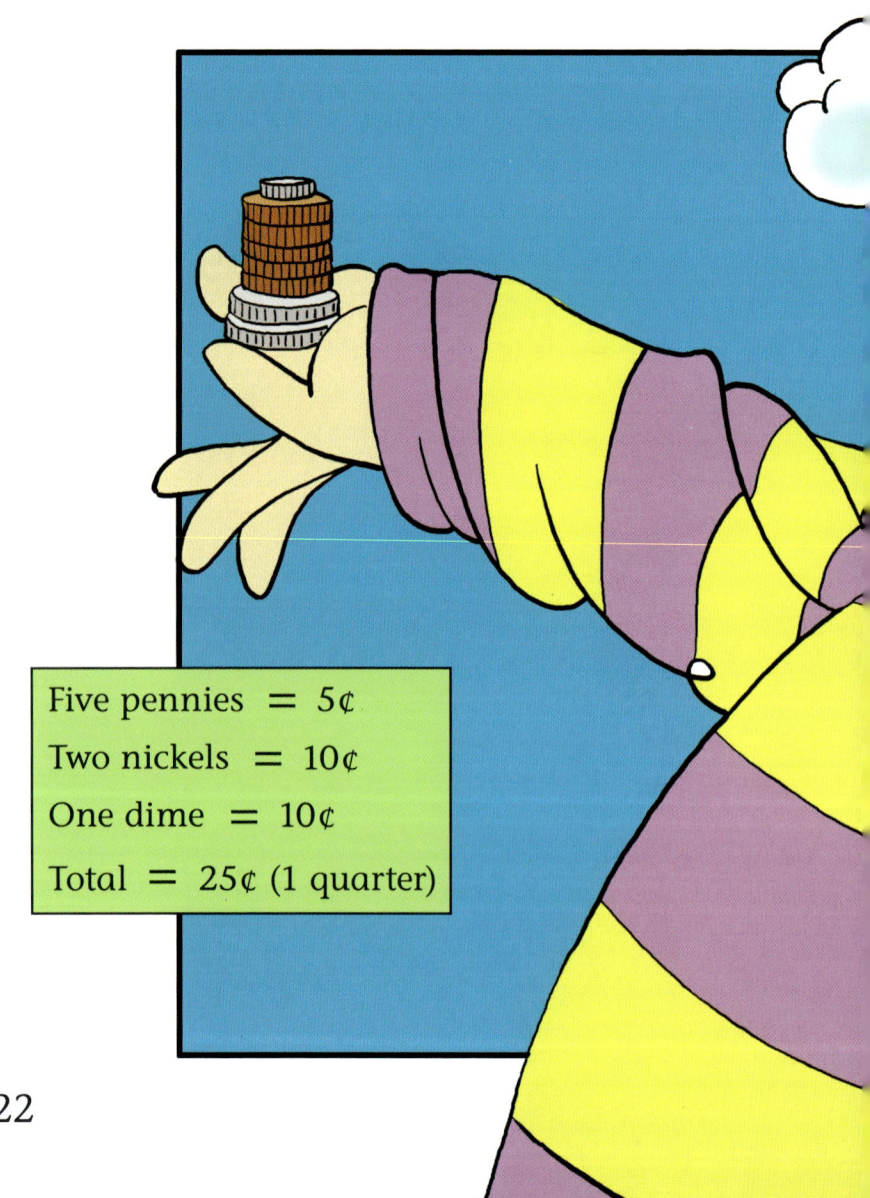

Five pennies = 5¢
Two nickels = 10¢
One dime = 10¢
Total = 25¢ (1 quarter)

"Can I play one more game?" she asked her mom.

"Just one more," her mom said. "Then it's time to go."

Jody used her change to buy her last ticket. She decided to play the spinning wheel game. She didn't know what number to put her ticket on.

Jody decided to put the ticket on number five. That was the same as the number of people in her family.

The girl at the booth spun the wheel. It spun around and around. Then it stopped on number five!

Jody jumped up and down. Jody's mom and dad clapped.

"What prize do you want?" asked the girl.

"Freddy the frog!" they all said together.

Jody handed Max the big green frog. Max hugged Freddy tight. Then he hugged Jody tight.

COUNTING MONEY ACTIVITY

Have a garage sale with your friends! Each friend gathers five toys, books, and other items that aren't used anymore. Using a sticker or tag, put an amount on each item (ex. 50¢, $1.00). Bring all the items together and see what you can sell to each other. Add up all the money. How much did each of you make?

GLOSSARY

dime—a coin worth ten cents
dollar—a unit of money worth one hundred cents
nickel—a coin worth five cents
penny—a coin worth one cent
quarter—a coin worth twenty-five cents

TO LEARN MORE

More Books to Read

Harris, Trudy. *Jenna Found a Penny.* Brookfield, CT: Millbrook Press, 2007.

Marrewa, Jennifer. *Using Money on a Shopping Trip.* Chappaqua, NY: Weekly Reader, 2007.

Rozines Roy, Jennifer. *Money at the Store.* New York: Tarrytown, N.Y: Benchmark Books, 2006.

Pistoia, Sara. *Money.* Mankato, MN: Child's World, 2006.

Dalton, Julie. *Counting Money.* Danbury CT: Children's Press, 2006.

On the Web

FactHound offers a safe, fun way to find Web sites related to topics in this book. All of the sites on FactHound have been researched by our staff.

1. Visit *www.facthound.com*
2. Type in this special code: 1404852514
3. Click on the FETCH IT button.

Your trusty FactHound will fetch the best sites for you!

LOOK FOR MORE BOOKS iN THE *READ-iT!* READERS: MATH SERIES:

Color Me Even, Color Me Odd (even and odd numbers)
The Guessing Game (weight)
The Lemonade Standoff (two-digit addition without regrouping)
Mike's Mystery (two-digit subtraction without regrouping)
The Pizza Palace (fractions)
The Pool Party (temperature)
Shells Alive (two-digit addition with regrouping)
The Tallest Snowman (measurements)
Too Many Tomatoes (two-digit subtraction with regrouping)